Zeb

Saddle Up Series
Book 60

Dave and Pat Sargent are longtime residents of Prairie Grove, Arkansas. Dave, a fourth-generation dairy farmer, began writing in early December 1990. Pat, a former teacher, began writing in the fourth grade. They enjoy the outdoors and have a real love for animals.

Zeb

Saddle Up Series
Book 60

By Dave and Pat Sargent

Beyond "The End"
By Sue Rogers

Illustrated by Jane Lenoir

Ozark Publishing, Inc.
P.O. Box 228
Prairie Grove, AR 72753

Cataloging-in-Publication Data

Sargent, Dave, 1941–
  Zeb / by Dave and Pat Sargent ; illustrated
by Jane Lenoir.—Prairie Grove, AR :
Ozark Publishing, c2004.
      p. cm. (Saddle up series ; 60)

      "Be prepared"—Cover.
      SUMMARY: By helping his boss lady
prepare small children to start school for
the first time, Zeb the zebra dun is involved in
inventing the first kindergarten.
      ISBN 1-56763-717-5 (hc)
            1-56763-718-3 (pbk)

      1. Horses—Juvenile fiction. [1. Kindergarten—
Fiction. 2. Schools—Fiction. 3. Horses—
Fiction.] I. Sargent, Pat, 1936– II. Lenoir,
Jane, 1950– ill. III. Title. IV. Series.

      PZ7.S2465Ze 2004
      [Fic]—dc21   2001005629

Printed in the United States of America

Inspired by

zebra duns we see beside the roads.

Dedicated to

all children who were, at one time, five years old and in kindergarten.

Foreword

When Zeb the zebra dun and his lady boss, Miss Annie Trebble, take a trip around the community visiting families with small children who are too young to start school, good things begin happening. Zeb helps Miss Annie start a program they call Kindergarten.

Contents

One   A Teacher for Little Ones   1

Two   Respect the Schoolmarm   11

Three   I'll Call It Kindergarten!   25

Four   Zebra Dun Facts   35

If you would like to have the authors of the Saddle Up Series visit your school, free of charge, call 1-800-321-5671 or 1-800-960-3876.

One

A Teacher for Little Ones

The moon was full and rising above the trees as crickets sang their cheerful song to the summer night. A big-eyed owl was perched on a limb near the front porch of the large white house. Zeb the zebra dun looked at him before slowly walking toward the front yard. "Hmmm," he thought. "I see that my boss lady is sitting outside this evening. I'll visit with her before I go to sleep."

"Evening, Boss," he nickered softly as he approached the porch.

"And how are you this fine night?"

Annie Trebble's hands were covering her face and her shoulders were trembling slightly.

"Oh mercy," Zeb groaned. "I think Boss Lady is feeling sad." He nuzzled her soft cheek with his lip. "Are you okay?" he asked.

Annie moved her hands from her face. A large tear trickled down her cheek, and she quickly wiped it away with one hand.

"Oh, Zeb, I wish you could talk," she whispered quietly. "I want to be a schoolteacher so badly, but Watertown, Wisconsin doesn't need me. They already have a fine man to teach the children."

"Hmmm, Boss," Zeb whinnied. "I think that anyone who wants to work with kids as much as you can surely find a way to do it."

Suddenly a woman appeared in the moonlight. She was walking at a fast pace toward the house. Her long skirt made a rustling sound as she hurried up the front-porch steps.

"Good evening, Mrs. Wilson," Annie said. "This is a nice surprise. I'm so glad that you came to visit. Would you like a cup of hot tea?"

Zeb thought it was a bit late in the day for a social call. He snorted

softly and backed away from the
front porch.

Mrs. Wilson sat down beside Annie and said, "I don't care for any tea, thank you, Miss Trebble. I'm hoping you may be able to help me with my son."

Zeb pawed the ground with one front hoof and murmured, "A real problem kid, huh? I don't want to sound bad or mean, but Boss Lady has problems of her own right now."

"Danny?" Annie asked quickly. "Is he all right?"

"Yes," Mrs. Wilson replied with a smile, "except he is so bored. That boy is constantly asking questions, and I don't know the answers. He's not old enough for the first grade, but his mind is ready to learn."

"I see," Annie said. "Have you asked the teacher about enrolling him early?"

Zeb shook his head. His ears were pointed forward as he moved closer to the two ladies.

"Now this," he thought, "sounds like opportunity knocking!"

Mrs. Wilson pushed a lock of hair back from her eyes and said with a sigh, "The teacher would not even consider the idea. He said that Danny is just too young and would disrupt the other students."

"He's a bright boy," Annie said. After a brief moment of silence, she patted Mrs. Wilson on the arm and added, "I do like Danny. Give me a little time to think about this, okay?"

Mrs. Wilson smiled and then nodded her head. "I was hoping you could work with him, Miss Trebble."

A short time later, Mrs. Wilson left, and Annie leaned back in the porch swing with a thoughtful expression on her face.

Zeb pawed the ground again and nickered softly, "Boss Lady, let's think about this."

He felt happy when Boss Annie suddenly smiled. She walked down the porch steps and hugged his neck.

"Maybe there's a place for me after all, Zeb," she said softly. "Maybe I will work in the field of education with little ones."

Zeb felt warm fuzzies of love and happiness as he nickered softly, "Life is wonderful."

Two

Respect the Schoolmarm

The sun was peeking over the eastern horizon when Zeb heard a familiar voice.

"Oh what a beautiful morning!" Annie proclaimed as she skipped into the barn.

"Wow, Boss Lady," the zebra dun nickered, "you sound happy. What do you have in mind for us to do today?"

As she poured oats in Zeb's manger Miss Annie said, "I feel that other young children may have the same questions as Danny. We are going to visit some parents, Zeb."

"Good idea," Zeb muttered as he munched on his grain. "As soon as I finish eating we'll get started."

Annie quickly gathered up the bridle, blanket, and sidesaddle. As the zebra dun opened his mouth for another bite of oats, she quickly slipped the bit between his teeth.

"Sorry, Zeb," she said with a cheerful laugh. "But there's no time to waste this morning. You'll have to finish your breakfast later. We have many miles to travel."

Zeb shook his head and pawed the stall with his front hoof.

"I'm not too sure this teacher thing is a good idea," he fumed.

Before he had a chance to go into detail, he was already saddled and being led from the barn.

Annie patted the zebra dun's neck before she put her left foot in the stirrup and sat down on the seat of the sidesaddle with her right leg nestled in the holder. She quickly smoothed the folds in her long skirt, and the black cloth cascaded over the left side of the horse. After straightening her posture, she again gave her best friend three or four comforting pats on the neck and then gently nudged him with her heel.

"Hmmm," Zeb murmured with a smile. "You know what I think? I think we make a pretty striking pair, Boss Lady!"

An hour later, Zeb and his boss, Miss Annie Trebble, were crossing an old wooden bridge when a deep voice bellowed from beneath it.

"Hey! You up there! Don't be so noisy!" it demanded. "I'm taking a nap in the shade of the bridge."

Zeb the zebra dun pawed at the planks.

"You shouldn't be so grouchy," he whinnied. "Boss Lady and I are too busy to wait until you have had your nap."

An agitated apricot linebacked dun suddenly peered over the edge of the bridge.

"My boss said to be quiet," the dun snorted. "You should back off and go to the next crossing."

Zeb snorted back at him. "And you should mind your manners.

Boss Lady and I have work to do."

A large man with a scruffy beard suddenly appeared from beneath the shade of the bridge. He walked up the bank of the creek and stepped onto the wooden planks.

"I think you need to be taught a lesson," he sneered.

His gaze shifted from Zeb to Miss Annie. A slow ornery smile appeared on his face as he took a step toward her.

"You sure are a pretty gal," he sputtered. "I'd like to get to know you better."

"Stay away from me," Annie warned.

"I may look rough, little lady," the man snarled, "but you'll like me once you get to know me."

Zeb glared at the apricot line-backed dun and said, "Get your boss away from my boss lady before I hurt him."

The apricot linebacked dun said, "You're not big enough or mean enough to handle my boss. He does what he wants, when he wants to do it."

The man took two steps toward
Annie. His hand was grabbing for
her when Zeb whirled and kicked.

"Hang on, Boss," he murmured as his two hind feet connected with the man's big belly.

The fellow let out an "Oomph" as he staggered around. Seconds later, he fell backward off the bridge and landed in the creek. Ker-splash!

Zeb looked at the apricot line-backed dun and said, "I suggest that you teach your boss some manners. He should treat a schoolmarm with proper respect."

The dun glanced at his soaking-wet disgruntled boss. A big clump of muddy moss was on top of his head.

"I think," the dun murmured, "that you already taught him that."

"Very well," Zeb nickered as he trotted proudly across the bridge.

Three

I'll Call It Kindergarten!

Zeb the zebra dun and Annie visited several families that day. The Smith family had a little girl who was five years old and very inquisitive.

As they left the Smith farm, Annie said, "I have two students, Zeb. Isn't it wonderful?"

"That's good," the zebra dun whinnied. "And we have visited only four homes so far."

Around thirty minutes later, they came to a halt beside a grey sabino who was pulling a big wagon.

"Howdy," Zeb said. "Does your boss have any children?"

The grey sabino nodded his head.

"He sure does. He and his wife have six. Three girls and three boys." Then the sabino added, "One boy and one girl are twins. Those two keep us all busy."

"How old are they?" Zeb asked. "My boss lady is a teacher, and she is wanting to teach five-year-olds before they are able to enroll in the first grade."

"Perfect!" the sabino nickered. "Susie and Joe Bill just had their fifth birthday. Tell your boss lady that I wish her luck. Those two are a handful."

Moments later, Zeb broke into a lope. Miss Annie laughed and urged him to go faster. Soon the happy schoolmarm and the zebra dun were racing beneath the cool shade of the trees.

"Life is so wonderful!" Annie laughed with delight as Zeb slowed to a trot and finally came to a halt beside a cool spring of water.

"I'm so happy that you're going to teach little kids," Zeb murmured. "You will be a fine schoolmarm."

Annie dismounted and sat down on the cool grass beneath a big shade tree. The zebra dun munched on the green foliage as Annie quietly began to doze. "Hmmm," he thought. "I'm sure glad we stopped to rest for a while. I had forgotten that I didn't finish my breakfast this morning."

Around thirty minutes later, Annie suddenly awoke. She stood up and quickly began to pace back and forth in front of the zebra dun. His head followed her movement right to left and left to right as she nervously walked.

"Wait! Hold it!" he suddenly nickered. "You're driving me crazy. What's the matter?"

"Oh, Zeb," she blurted. "I want to teach little ones, but I want my education to count."

Annie continued, "I want to get them prepared for their grade-school days, but I want to teach them data and subjects that they can use when they enter first grade. My work is not going to be recognized as proper instruction for these little ones unless a program is recognized and accepted by the school."

The zebra dun cocked his head to one side and looked at Annie for several moments without comment. "It's kind of hard," he thought, "to give suggestions to my boss lady when I don't even understand the problem. So I'll just nuzzle her on the cheek, rather than say anything that she might think is silly."

"This pre-school instruction needs a name, Zeb," Annie said. "It needs a term that signifies a part of the education system. But what? What could it be?"

"How about Learning Young?" the zebra dun nickered. "Or maybe Kinda Early?"

"Hmmm," Annie said. "Kinder something would work." She shook her head and said, "Kindergarten." Excitement glistened within her eyes as she repeated, "Kindergarten. That's it! I'll call it Kindergarten!"

"Hmmm," Zeb thought as he watched his boss lady dance happily near the little pool of water. "This Kindergarten idea just may go down in history as little children begin their education at a younger age. But I wonder if folks will remember a zebra dun horse named Zeb who helped Boss Lady Annie Trebble. It doesn't matter. Life is great and just getting better and better!"

Four

Zebra Dun Facts

Some cowboys use the term *dun* for yellow horses with black points. Some cowboys use the term *dun* to describe all of the lighter horse colors, some of which do not have black points. According to cowboys, duns tend to have points darker than the body color. The base of the tail and sides of the mane are lighter than the remaining tail and mane hairs.

Cowboys call yellow-coated horses with black points buckskins.

When primitive marks are present, cowboys call them zebra duns. This is the color most refer to as dun, but the term zebra dun allows for more detail and less confusion.

Zebra Dun

BEYOND "THE END"

*Riding: The art of keeping
a horse between you and the ground.*
The London Times

WORD LIST
zebra dun
bridle
hay
wide-toothed metal comb
blanket
apricot linebacked dun
hoof pick
saddle
grey sabino
sweat scraper
oats
rubber currycombs
Quarter Horse
stirrup

chestnut
salt
halter
roan

From the word list above, write:

1. Five words that name color of horses.

2. Five words that name tack for horses.

3. Four words that name grooming tools. Tell what each one is used for.

4. Three words that name food for a horse.

5. One word that names a breed of horse.

CURRICULUM CONNECTIONS

When it has been in a stable all winter without grass, a horse should be allowed to graze only a short time each day. Why is this?

Three horses have just reached the age of a mare, a stallion, and aged. How many total years have they lived?

Miss Annie Trebble had a very good idea. Do you like the name she and Zeb decided to name kindergarten? If it needed a different name, what would you suggest?

The most important goal of kindergarten is to get kindergartners ready for elementary school. Think back to the year you were in kindergarten. Make a list of the things you learned that year that have helped you to succeed in elementary school.

PROJECT

Combine your math and artistic skills! Draw to scale and accurately color a picture (body, tail, and mane) of the horse that is featured in each book read in the Saddle Up Series. You could soon have sixty horses prancing around the walls of your classroom!

Learning + horses = FUN.

Look in your school library media center for books about how to draw a horse and the colors of horses. Don't forget the useful information in the last chapter of this book (Zebra Dun Facts) and the picture on the book cover for a shape and color guide.

HELPFUL HINTS AND WEBSITES

A horse is measured in hands. One hand equals four inches. Use a scale of 1" equals 1 hand.

Visit website <www.equisearch.com> to find a glossary of equine terms, information about tack and equipment, breeds, art and graphics, and more about horses. Learn more at <www.horse-country. com> and at <www.ansi.okstate.edu/ breeds/horses/>.

KidsClick! is a web search for kids by librarians. There are many interesting websites here. HORSES and HORSE- MANSHIP are two of the more than 600 subjects. Visit <www.kidsclick.org>.

Is your classroom beginning to look like the Rocking S Horse Ranch? Happy Trails to You!

ANSWERS (1. If a horse has not been used to eating grass, eating too much all at once, especially wet clover, could give the horse colic. 2. 16 years.)